MW00929694

Contents

Ikki's Warning

Long ago, before Mowgli left the Seeonee Jungle, he was playing with Pappu, the red panda, under a tree.

Soon Baloo came there and scolded Mowgli for giving his lessons a miss that day.

Mowgli felt ashamed and apologised, "Baloo, I forgot, I'm sorry!"

Baloo sat beside him. Mowgli asked, "Baloo, do all the animals follow the Jungle Law?"

Baloo said, "Yes, they do. However, there are a few who don't bother about the laws. But they suffer, sooner or later."

After a while, Ikki, the porcupine, came to Baloo. He said, "Baloo, all the yams in the jungle are drying up. It is not a good omen. Something bad is going to happen!"

Mowgli laughed at Ikki and said, "Baloo, this little creature is trying to pretend to be wiser than us. Send him away!"

Mowgli's behaviour irritated Ikki and he left.

Baloo said, "Mowgli, wisdom has nothing to do with size. Ikki is wiser than many big animals here."

Mowgli realised he was wrong. He went to Ikki and apologised. Ikki accepted his apology, and they went their separate ways.

No Spring In The Jungle

It was springtime in the Seeonee Jungle. However, not a single flower had bloomed.

One day, Mowgli met Baloo and said, "Let's sit under the shade of your favourite Mahua tree and study."

Baloo agreed and they went to the Mahua tree, only to discover that it also had no leaves.

Mowgli asked, "The Mahua looks so dull and dry. What is wrong, Baloo?"

A worried Baloo said, "Mowgli, do you remember about Ikki's warning a few days ago, that the yams in the jungle were drying? Like the yams, the trees are also drying. Bad times are coming. I'm worried!"

Mowgli said, "Baloo, I went to the river in the morning. The water in the river is much less than it used to be. The grass is drying and turning yellow. Is there going to be a drought this year?"

Baloo nodded and said, "It has not rained this year. The entire jungle will suffer from water shortage. We must have a meeting soon. Let's call all our friends."

Mowgli said, "Yes. Let's do that. As it is late now, we will have the meeting tomorrow morning."

Mowgli's Friends Support Him

The next morning, Mowgli gathered the members of his pack and a few others for the meeting with Baloo.

After everyone arrived, Baloo said, "It has not rained this year and the temperature is rising continuously. The heat has dried up most of the ponds in the jungle."

Bagheera said, "The condition of the plants and trees is also very bad. Most of them are drying and turning yellow."

Pappu asked, "What does all this indicate, Baloo?"

Baloo replied, "Our jungle is suffering from a severe drought. Soon, we will have nothing to eat and drink."

Mowgli asked, "Is there any way we can save our lives?"

Baloo said, "No. Going to another jungle will

mean fighting for hunting grounds with the animals there. Moreover, the beasts in the other jungle will never spare Mowgli's life."

Bagheera agreed with Baloo. He said, "I cannot risk Mowgli's life. I am staying here with him."

Akela declared, "Any wolf who wants to leave is free to go. However, I will stay and die in the place where I was born and grew up."

Mowgli thanked Baloo, Bagheera and Akela. They decided to support each other in difficult times.

Mowgli Begins To Starve

During the drought, Mowgli searched for food for many days. He could not find anything. He became thin and weak, but asked no one for help.

One day, Mowgli went to the river and sat there. He thought, 'I am sure I will die soon. I have never suffered such weakness before!'

After a while, Bagheera came by. He said, "Mowgli, you look very weak. Have you eaten anything?"

Mowgli said nothing, but a few tears fell on his cheeks.

Bagheera understood and said, "You are starving. I killed a bullock yesterday. Come, let's eat."

Mowgli went with Bagheera and ate the bullock. Then, Bagheera took him to Baloo and said, "Mowgli will not be able to find animals to hunt during the drought. Is there anything else he can live on?"

Baloo loved Mowgli a lot. He could not bear to see him in this terrible state. He said, "Mowgli, I know some trees where the honey bees store their honey. It is stale but nutritious. You can climb those trees easily."

Then, Baloo took Mowgli to those trees. There were old beehives on each one of them. Mowgli thanked Baloo and Bagheera for their kindness.

Hathi Proclaims Water Truce

One day, Mowgli had gone to drink water, when he saw a rock in the middle of the river. He wondered, 'I have never seen this rock before. Where has it come from?'

After a while, Hathi, the elephant, came there. He was the oldest living animal in the jungle.

Mowgli asked him, "Hathi, have you ever seen this rock before?"

Hathi replied, "This rock was always in the river. It is called the 'Peace Rock'. Earlier, the water covered it. Since the water level in the river is decreasing day by day, the rock is visible now."

Mowgli said, "It is an alarming situation."

Hathi said, "It is certainly a testing time for all of us. I must declare the water truce, at once."

Mowgli asked, "What is the water truce?"

Hathi replied, "When there is water scarcity,

the water truce means that it is against the Jungle Law to kill animals near a water body."

Then, Hathi lifted up his trunk as per the tradition. He loudly trumpeted ten times to proclaim the water truce.

Mowgli went to inform his friends about the water truce. He did not want anybody to break the law by mistake.

A Meeting In The Jungle

All the animals learnt about the proclamation of the water truce. So, by evening, they gathered for a meeting near the river.

Hathi said, "I have proclaimed the water truce. Until it rains, no one will kill animals that come to the river to drink water."

Bagheera said, "We, flesh eaters, will suffer a lot, as we hunt mostly near the river."

Hathi said, "This is the Jungle Law and no one can change it."

Bagheera understood and kept quiet.

Mowgli asked Hathi, "The rain seems to have forgotten us. Will we all die?"

Hathi replied, "This bad time will pass. The rain will soon fall and bring happiness to the entire jungle."

After a while, Sher Khan came to the river. He

saw the animals and said, "Ah! A meeting of all the animals without their king, Sher Khan! This is not fair!"

Baloo said, "You were never our king, O Lame Tiger. Go away!"

Then, all the animals declared together, "Hathi is the wisest. He is our chief."

Sher Khan knew that no one would listen to him, so he drank water and went away.

Tha, The First Elephant

Mowgli was surprised that Sher Khan behaved well with Hathi. He said, "Hathi, I am amazed to see Sher Khan being so polite with you!"

Hathi replied, "Sher Khan knows my strength. He respects me for another reason. There is a long story behind it, Mowgli."

Mowgli requested, "Hathi, please tell us the story!"

Many animals gathered at the riverside, when they heard that Hathi was going to narrate a story. Hathi leisurely sat on a rock and narrated a very old jungle tale.

According to Hathi, Tha, an elephant, was the first to arrive on Earth. He was so strong that he pulled the present jungle out of deep waters.

Then, Tha made rivers and ponds in it for the animals. Slowly, more animals arrived. Tha

had the responsibility of managing everybody. Slowly, his work became too much to handle. So, he delegated some work to First Tiger, who had arrived after him.

Thus, First Tiger became Tha's subordinate. The present elephants and tigers are Tha's and First Tiger's descendants. Tha's children are superior to First Tiger's children. Therefore, Hathi is superior to Sher Khan and commands his respect.

All the animals enjoyed listening to the story.

The Golden Times

One day, Hathi was sitting in the water near the Peace Rock to escape the heat, when Mowgli came there to drink water. Mowgli said, "Hathi, tell us some more about your ancestor Tha."

Hathi replied, "Curious little boy! All right."

Other animals also gathered around them. Hathi began, "During Tha's times, the animals had never seen or heard of men. No animal was killed for food. Even the beasts lived on plants, leaves and fruits. Even the tigers ate fruit and grass like other animals."

Bagheera frowned, "I would have hated to eat fruits!"

Hathi disliked being interrupted. He gave Bagheera a sharp look, and continued, "After a while, the animals began to fight with each other over food. There were enough grazing grounds for all, but they became lazy. Each wished to eat where he lay."

Suddenly, the tale was interrupted by the sound of thunder. The animals rejoiced as they felt it was going to rain. Hathi promised to continue the tale later. All the animals ran for shelter. Mowgli was a little disappointed, but nevertheless, went back to his cave.

The First Tiger's Tale

The sky had darkened with clouds. It thundered and a few drops of rain fell on the ground. Suddenly, the sky cleared up. The hungry and disappointed animals gathered again near the river.

Hathi continued Tha's tale, "Tha was busy making new jungles when disputes arose amongst the animals. He could not walk to all places to settle the disputes. Therefore, he made First Tiger the judge."

Mowgli asked, "How did First Tiger look like?"

Hathi replied, "He was as large as I am, and very beautiful. He was yellow in colour. He had no stripes. He also ate fruits and grass. None of the animals feared him."

Baloo asked, "Then, what happened to him that he became so fierce?"

18

Hathi replied, "One day, two deer were fighting. First Tiger was sleeping in the bushes. By mistake, one of the deer poked him with his horn. First Tiger became very angry. He forgot that he was the judge and killed the deer."

Baloo exclaimed, "Oh! What a terrible thing to happen in a peaceful jungle!"

Hathi replied, "Yes, Baloo. This was the first death in the jungle."

How Tigers Got Their Stripes

One day, Sher Khan came to the river. He saw Mowgli sitting alone on a rock. He thought, 'It's a brilliant opportunity to kill him!'

So, he charged towards him. However, as he neared Mowgli, he was startled to see many other animals, including Hathi, sitting by the riverside. So, he quietly drank water and went away.

Mowgli saw Sher Khan and the black stripes on his coat. So, he asked Hathi, "How did the tigers get the black stripes?"

Hathi replied, "First Tiger killed a deer in rage. Thus, he let 'death' loose in the jungle. Other animals informed Tha about the deer's death, but no one knew who caused it. So, Tha ordered the tree branches to bend low and mark the killer's body with stripes when he crossed their path."

Mowgli asked, "Did the branches mark First Tiger's coat?"

Hathi replied, "Yes. These are the stripes that First Tiger's successors will carry forever."

Mowgli asked, "How did Tha punish First Tiger?"

Hathi said, "Tha took all his power and sent him away to live alone."

All the animals were happy that First Tiger was punished. They thanked Hathi for telling them such interesting tales.

21

First Tiger Begins To Eat Flesh

One day, Mowgli was very hungry. The drought had destroyed all the plants and he was starving for many days. He met Baloo and said, "I have drunk all the honey that you showed me. Is there any more?"

Baloo took Mowgli to the outskirts of the jungle. There, he showed him a few more trees where the bees had stored their honey.

On their way back, Mowgli asked Baloo, "According to Hathi, First Tiger earlier ate leaves and fruits. Why did he start eating flesh, Baloo?"

Baloo smiled and said, "A man's curiosity can never be satisfied! The trees, while obeying Tha's orders, marked First Tiger's coat with stripes. So, First Tiger took this as an insult and vowed not to eat from the trees."

"Then, how did he live?" Mowgli asked.

"Hunger pangs drove First Tiger mad. He starting killing whatever came his way, especially the weaker animals. His children and all who followed them did the same," Baloo said.

Mowgli felt sad and said, "If First Tiger could have controlled his temper, all the animals would have been living peacefully today."

Baloo agreed with him.

Hathi Scolds Sher Khan

One day, Mowgli was going to the outskirts of the jungle in search of honey. Midway, he met Hathi. A curious Mowgli asked, "Where are you going, Hathi?"

Hathi said, "I cannot find a single green leaf to eat in the jungle. So, I thought of searching elsewhere. Maybe there is some greenery still left where the jungle ends."

Mowgli asked, "Can I also come with you?"

Hathi offered to take him on his back. Mowgli was delighted, and sat on his back. On the way, they met Sher Khan.

Hathi said, "Sher Khan, you have blood all over your face. What have you done?"

Sher Khan replied, "I had gone to the village last night. I killed a man and ate him."

Hathi said, "You should be ashamed of yourself.

Killing men is cowardice. Men will hunt you and kill you. Such a shameful death would be a perfect punishment for your evil deeds!"

Sher Khan replied, "But, I was starving for many days!"

Hathi grew angrier and said, "Most of the jungle beasts are starving due to drought. But none of them dared to sin like you. Go away!"

Sher Khan felt deeply insulted. But, he quietly went away.

First Tiger Brings Fear To Jungle

The drought seemed never ending. Since there was nothing to hunt, Baloo, Bagheera and many other carnivores gathered to hear Hathi's tales.

One day, Baloo asked Hathi, "What happened to First Tiger after Tha banished him from the forest?"

Hathi replied, "One day, First Tiger saw a cave. A man came out and stared at him. The man's eyes scared First Tiger and he ran to Tha. Tha told him that he had brought 'death' to the jungle by killing the deer. With death came 'fear' in the form of man."

Mowgli asked, "Are tigers afraid of men?"

Hathi replied, "Yes, they are. If tigers challenge men from the front, they will lose. So, they always try to catch men unawares."

Mowgli requested Hathi to continue the tale.

So, Hathi said, "First Tiger wanted to kill 'fear'. Therefore, he killed the man in the cave and earned the anger of men. Men started to come to the jungle and killed not only the tigers, but also other animals. First Tiger was also killed by a man, a few days later."

The animals cursed First Tiger for bringing 'death' to the jungle.

Then, they went to their shelters to rest.

Heavy Rains Lash The Jungle

As the drought continued, the river in the jungle had very little water in it. The jungle turned brown in colour with dried grass. Many animals had died of hunger and thirst. It grew hotter day by day.

The animals, who were alive, wondered how long they would live. Baloo said to Bagheera,

"We don't have a choice. We must leave this jungle. Otherwise, we will die soon!"

Bagheera agreed and said, "Look at us. So thin, and all our bones are sticking out! But, I am really worried about Mowgli. Will he be able to survive in another place?"

Baloo said, "He has fainted due to hunger. I wonder how long he will live if he does not eat!"

They cried as they looked at Mowgli, who was lying unconscious under a dead tree. Suddenly, they saw a big black cloud cover the sun. They looked longingly at it and wished that it would rain.

Mowgli woke up when some drops of water fell on his face. He was shocked to see it was raining!

Baloo and Bagheera ran towards him and they hugged each other. Baloo exclaimed, "Ah! Finally, it's raining!"

All the animals danced and thanked God for his blessing.

Happiness Returns To The Jungle

Heavy rains continued to lash the jungle for two consecutive weeks. All the water bodies were full again. Fishes, frogs and turtles filled the ponds and the river. Soon, the trees and plants became green, too. Everything was full of life again. Many animals returned to their homes.

One day, Akela, Mowgli and a few other wolves, those who had stayed back during the drought, were sitting near their meeting place.

After a while, they saw some wolves, who had left the jungle, pleading with Akela. They looked hurt, tired and hungry.

One of them said, "Dear Leader, we have been driven out from other jungles by the wolves there. So, we decided to come back. We are glad that our jungle is rich and green again."

Mowgli said, "Akela, we will not take them back in our pack! They left us in times of trouble."

However, the wolves pleaded, "We are starving. If you don't help us, we will die!"

Akela said, "Mowgli, I agree that these wolves left us in times of trouble. But, they are still our brothers. We cannot be mean to them."

Then, Akela invited all the wolves for a meal. Everybody thanked their leader for his kindness.

Available in the 15 Stories Series
A Great Series for Young Readers

For more details visit www.shreebookcentre.com